MAY 2023

WITH
April & Mae

SUNDAY

MONDAY

TUESDAY

WEDNESDAY

THURSDAY

FRIDAY

SATURDAY

Collect them ALL!

April & Mae

and the

Movie Night

THE SATURDAY BOOK

MEGAN DOWD LAMBERT

Illustrated by GISELA BOHÓRQUEZ

ini Charlesbridge

To my husband, Sean, who hates mushrooms
on pizza, likes science-fiction movies, and loves me
anyway. I love you with all my heart.—M. D. L.

To my uncle Jairo. Thanks for filling my world
with marvelous books.—G. B.

Text copyright © 2023 by Megan Dowd Lambert
Illustrations copyright © 2023 by Gisela Bohórquez
All rights reserved, including the right of reproduction in whole
or in part in any form. Charlesbridge and colophon are registered
trademarks of Charlesbridge Publishing, Inc.

At the time of publication, all URLs printed in this book were accurate
and active. Charlesbridge, the author, and the illustrator are not responsible
for the content or accessibility of any website.

Published by Charlesbridge
9 Galen Street, Watertown, MA 02472 • (617) 926-0329 • www.charlesbridge.com

Library of Congress Cataloging-in-Publication Data
Names: Lambert, Megan Dowd, author. | Bohórquez, Gisela, illustrator.
Title: April & Mae and the movie night: the Saturday book / Megan Dowd Lambert;
    illustrated by Gisela Bohórquez.
Other titles: April and Mae and the movie night
Description: Watertown, MA: Charlesbridge, [2023] | Series: Every day with April
    & Mae | Audience: Ages 5–8. | Summary: "April and Mae are best friends (and
    so are their pets). On Saturdays they have a movie night: Mae brings pizza she
    knows April will like and April picks a movie she knows Mae will like. When
    the movie is too scary for April, the friends realize that it is OK to like different
    things as long as they like each other."—Provided by publisher. |
Identifiers: LCCN 2021029000 (print) | LCCN 2021029001 (ebook) |
    ISBN 9781623542641 (hardcover) | ISBN 9781632898821 (ebook)
Subjects: LCSH: Best friends—Juvenile fiction. | Friendship—Juvenile fiction. |
    Choice (Psychology)—Juvenile fiction. | CYAC: Best friends—Fiction. |
    Friendship—Fiction. | Difference (Psychology)—Fiction. | Choice—Fiction. |
    LCGFT: Picture books.
Classification: LCC PZ7.1.L26 Al 2023 (print) | LCC PZ7.1.L26 (ebook) |
    DDC 813.6 [E]—dc23
LC record available at https://lccn.loc.gov/2021029000
LC ebook record available at https://lccn.loc.gov/2021029001

Printed in China
(hc) 10 9 8 7 6 5 4 3 2 1

The art herein is drawn in the style of the series characters originally
    illustrated by Briana Dengoue.
Illustrations done in Photoshop
Display type set in Jacoby by Adobe
Text type set in Grenadine by Markanna Studios Inc.
Printed by 1010 Printing International Limited in Huizhou, Guangdong, China
Production supervision by Jennifer Most Delaney
Designed by Cathleen Schaad

April and Mae
love movie nights.

Mae plans the food.
April does not.
April picks the movie.
Mae does not.
But April and Mae
are friends.
Best friends.

And their pets
are best friends, too.

One Saturday, movie night
is at April's house.
Mae brings her cat,
and snacks for the pets.
She brings pizza crust
and toppings, too.

"Yum!" says April.
"I like pineapple pizza!"
"I know," says Mae.
"That is why I got pineapple."
"But *you* do not like
    pineapple pizza," says April.

"I know," says Mae.

"That is why I got peppers, too."

"You can *try* pineapple pizza,"
 says April.

"No, thank you," says Mae.

"I like what I like."

They put the pizza in the oven.
Then April sees Mae's other bag.
"What is in that bag?" asks April.
"A secret," says Mae.
"Yay!" says April.
"I like secrets!"
"I know," says Mae.
"And you will like this one."

DING! goes the oven.

"Yum," says April.

"Yum," says Mae.

"Purr," says Mae's cat.

"Woof," says April's dog.

Now the pizza is gone.
The pet snacks are gone, too.

"That was the best pizza," says April.
"Is it time for the secret now?"
"No," says Mae.
"Now it is time for the movie."

"OK," says April.
She wants to pick
the best movie for Mae.
She takes a long, long time.

"Just pick," says Mae.

"I am trying," says April.

"I like all kinds of movies," says Mae.

"I know," says April.

April picks a scary movie.

"Yay!" says Mae.

"I like scary movies."

"I know," says April.

"That's why I picked it."

"But wait," says Mae.

"*You* do not like

scary movies."

"I know," says April.

"But I can *try* to like this one."

April starts the movie.

Mae stops the movie.

"Are you sure you want
 to try this movie?" asks Mae.

"I *do* like dog movies," says April.

"That is not a dog," says Mae.

"That is a werewolf."

"I know," says April.

"OK," says Mae.

April sits with her dog.
Mae sits with her cat.
April tries to like the movie.

She tries

and tries.

But April does *not* like it.

"Aaaah!" yells April.

"Meooow!" yells Mae's cat.

Mae stops the movie.

"Are you OK, April?" asks Mae.

"Yes," says April.

"Then why are you under the table?" asks Mae.

"I lost something," says April.

"What did you lose?" asks Mae.

"My nerve!" says April.

April gets up.

Mae looks at her friend.

Mae looks at her cat under the chair.

"My cat lost his nerve, too," says Mae.

"I am sorry," says April.
"Why?" asks Mae.
"You are my friend," says April.
"I am sorry we do not like
all the same movies."

"Friends do not have to
   like all the same things,"
   says Mae.
"They do not?" asks April.
"No," says Mae.
"Friends just have to like each other."

"I like you, Mae," says April.

"I like you, too, April," says Mae.

"Even if I do not like scary movies?" asks April.

"Yes!" says Mae.

"You like what you like."

The friends hug.

Mae's cat comes out

from under the chair.

April's dog wags his tail.

"I *do* like this movie," says Mae.
"Do you want to watch the rest?"
  asks April.
"Yes!" says Mae.
"OK. I will wait in the kitchen,"
  says April.
"Save some milk and
  cookies for me," says Mae.

"Is that the secret?" asks April.

"Yes!" says Mae.

"Yay!" says April.

"Cookies are my favorite kind of secret."

"Mine, too," says Mae.

"I will take your cat
with me," says April.
"I will keep your dog
with me," says Mae.

April goes to the kitchen
with Mae's cat.
Mae watches the scary movie
with April's dog.

April chews cookies.
Mae's cat purrs.
The wind blows.
The clock ticks.
Then, "ROAR!"
Mae yells, "Aaah!"
"Woof, woof,
woof!" barks
April's dog.

Now it is very quiet.
April's nerve is lost again.
"Are you OK, Mae?" calls April
from under the table.

"Meow?" calls Mae's cat
from under the chair.

"This scary movie is so fun," says Mae.

Mae comes into the kitchen
with April's dog.
"You picked the best movie!" says Mae.

"I am glad you liked it," says April.
"But please do not tell me about it."
"I will keep it a secret," says Mae.
"Thank you," says April.

The friends sit at the table.
Mae eats a cookie.
"We both like milk and cookies,"
Mae says.
"They go together," says April.
"Just like us."
"And like our pets," says Mae.
"And like pineapple pizza
and me," says April.
"And like scary movies
and me," says Mae.

And like reading books and *you.*